Being Your Be...

La mejor versión de...

Ducks Have Feelings

¡Los patos también tienen sentimientos!

David and Patricia Armentrout
Translation by Pablo de la Vega
David y Patricia Armentrout
Traducción de Pablo de la Vega

A Crabtree Seedlings Book
Un libro de El Semillero de Crabtree

Crabtree Publishing
crabtreebooks.com

Simon Zebra
Simón Cebra

Chester Fox   Chester Zorro

2

Sara Duck
Sara Pato

3

Sara felt her face turn red.
Sara sintió que se ponía roja.

8

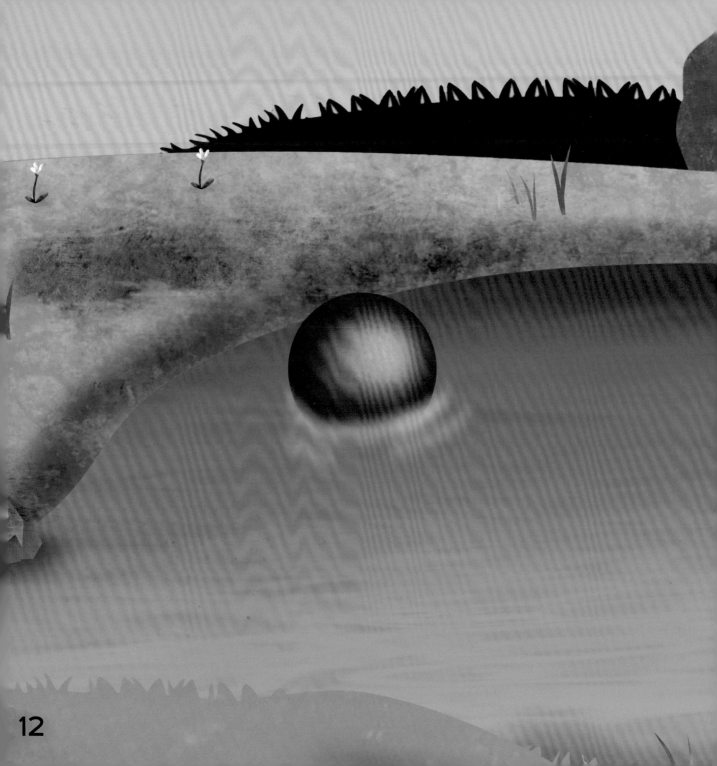

13

School-to-Home Support for Caregivers and Teachers

This book helps children grow by letting them practice reading. Here are a few guiding questions to help the reader build his or her comprehension skills. Possible answers appear here in red.

Before Reading

- **What do I think this book is about?** *I think this book is about a duck who got her feelings hurt. I think this book is about playing safe on the playground.*

- **What do I want to learn about this topic?** *I want to learn how to not get my feelings hurt when someone teases me. I want to learn how to be tough and not cry when someone teases me.*

During Reading

- **I wonder why...** *I wonder why Chester made fun of Sara's feet. I wonder why Sara's face turned red.*

- **What have I learned so far?** *I have learned that you can make people sad when you make fun of their feet. I have learned that ducks feet help them to swim.*

After Reading

- **What details did I learn about this topic?** *I have learned that you can hurt someone's feelings without trying to. I have learned that if you hurt someone's feelings you should always say you're sorry.*

- **Write down unfamiliar words and ask questions to help understand their meaning.** *I see the word* **kickball** *on page 4. I can tell it is a game. How do you play kickball? I also see the word* **felt** *on page 7. What does it mean?*

Written by David and Patricia Armentrout
Illustrated by Anita DuFalla
Prepress and print production coordinator: Katherine Berti

Crabtree Publishing

crabtreebooks.com   800-387-7650

Printed in Printed in China/082022/FE052422CT

Published in Canada
Crabtree Publishing
616 Welland Ave.
St. Catharines, Ontario
L2M 5V6

Published in the United States
Crabtree Publishing
347 Fifth Avenue,
Suite 1402-145
New York, NY, 10016

Library and Archives Canada Cataloguing in Publication
Available at the Library and Archives Canada

Library of Congress Cataloging-in-Publication Data
Available at the Library of Congress

Paperback: 9781039624719
Ebook: 9781039625556
Epub: 9781039625136